# Thesaurus Rex

Written by Laya Steinberg
Illustrated by Debbie Harter

**Barefoot Books**
*Celebrating Art and Story*

# Thesaurus Rex drinks his milk:
## sip, sup, swallow, swill.

and romp.

Wow! He's found a muddy swamp.

Thesaurus Rex starts to slip:

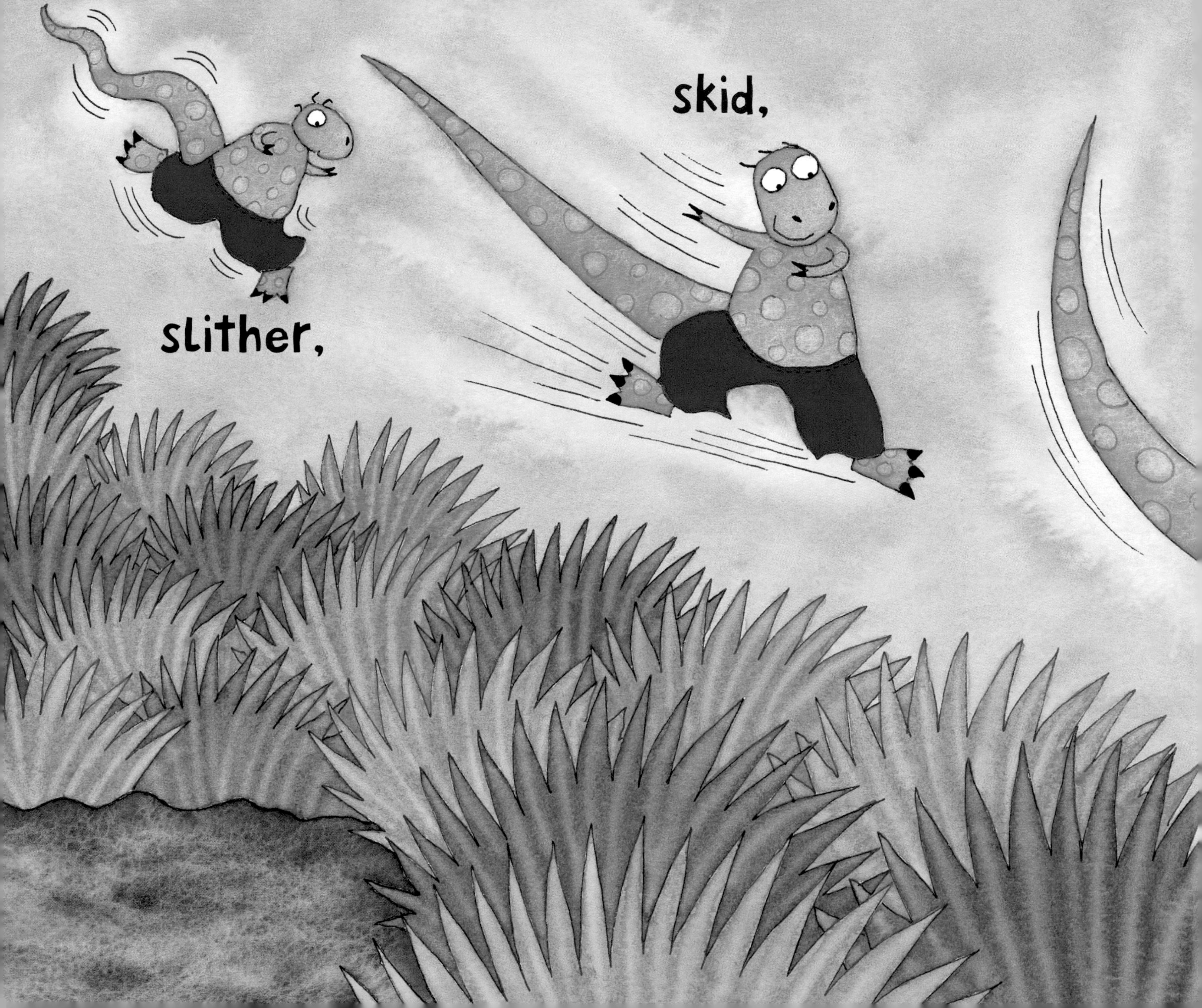

slither,

skid,

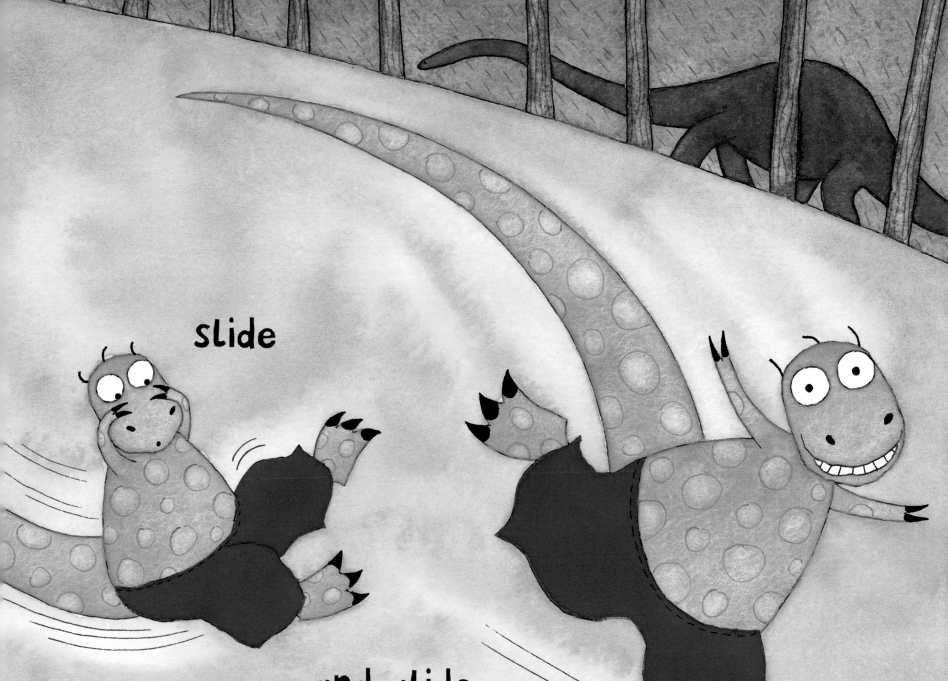

slide

and glide.

Whee! What a speedy ride!

Thesaurus Rex lands in mud:
slime, slush, mire and muck.

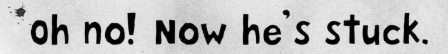

oh no! Now he's stuck.

Thesaurus Rex calls his Mum:
howl,
yowl,
squeal
and shout.

Whoosh, plop!
She pulls him out.

Thesaurus Rex must get clean:

wash,

bathe,

Thesaurus Rex is ready to eat:
munch, crunch, nibble, gnaw.

Chomp!
He likes his
dinner raw.

Thesaurus Rex leaps into bed:

bounces,

hurtles,

springs

and flies.

Tomorrow holds a new surprise.

Thesaurus Rex is all wrapped up:
bundled,
covered,
tucked in tight.

He'll have happy dreams tonight. Goodnight!

Barefoot Books
124 Walcot Street
Bath
BA1 5BG

First published in Great Britain in 2003 by Barefoot Books, Ltd.
This paperback edition first published in 2004

This book was typeset in Bokka
The illustrations were prepared in watercolour,
pen and ink and crayon on thick watercolour paper

Graphic design by Big Blu Ltd.
Colour separation by Grafiscan, Verona
Printed and bound in Hong Kong by South China Printing Co.

This book has been printed on 100% acid-free paper

3 5 7 9 8 6 4 2

Hardback ISBN 1-84148-054-1
Paperback ISBN 1-84148-787-2